Eliza Lee Cabot Follen

Twilight Stories - Little Songs

Eliza Lee Cabot Follen

Twilight Stories - Little Songs

ISBN/EAN: 9783744772990

Printed in Europe, USA, Canada, Australia, Japan

Cover: Foto ©Andreas Hilbeck / pixelio.de

More available books at **www.hansebooks.com**

Mrs. Follen's
Twilight Stories.

Mrs. Follen's

Twilight Stories

※

LITTLE SONGS

ILLUSTRATED

LEE & SHEPARD

BOSTON

BY

MRS. FOLLEN

Illustrated with above Fifty Pictures.

BOSTON 1889

LEE AND SHEPARD PUBLISHERS

10 MILK STREET NEXT "THE OLD SOUTH MEETING HOUSE"

NEW YORK CHAS. T. DILLINGHAM

718 AND 720 BROADWAY

PREFACE

TO THE FIRST AMERICAN EDITION.

It has been my object, in writing the following Little Songs for Little Boys and Girls, to endeavor to catch something of that good-humored pleasantry, that musical nonsense, which makes Mother Goose so attractive to children of all ages.

The little folks must decide whether the book is entertaining. To them I present my little volume, with the earnest hope that it will receive their approbation. If children love to lisp my rhymes, while parents find no fault in them, I ask no higher praise.

CAMBRIDGE, 1832.

(5)

PREFACE.

In the present edition of the "Nursery Songs," which has been carefully revised, the original name given by its parent and best friends is restored.

Two captivating little songs, by some unknown hand, appended to the English edition, are retained; and two or three from the first American edition, omitted in the English, are restored.

I will hope that the little folks will welcome the little book in its new dress, and make much of it; for it was at first made, and is now adorned with pictures, on purpose to please them.

ELIZA LEE FOLLEN.

BROOKLINE, MARCH 22, 1856.

(6)

CONTENTS.

LITTLE SONGS,

ANNIE'S GARDEN.

In little Annie's garden
   Grew all sorts of posies;
There were pinks, and mignonette,
   And tulips, and roses.

Sweet peas, and morning glories,
    A bed of violets blue,
And marigolds, and asters,
    In Annie's garden grew.

There the bees went for honey,
    And the humming-birds too;
And there the pretty butterflies
    And the lady-birds flew.

And there among her flowers,
    Every bright and pleasant day,
In her own pretty garden
    Little Annie went to play.

THE NEW MOON.

DEAR mother, how pretty
The moon looks to-night!
She was never so cunning before;

Her two little horns
Are so sharp and so bright,
I hope she'll not grow any more.

If I were up there
With you and my friends,
I'd rock in it nicely you see ;
I'd sit in the middle
And hold by both ends ;
O, what a bright cradle 'twould be !

I would call to the stars
To keep out of the way,
Lest we should rock over their toes,
And there I would rock
Till the dawn of the day,
And see where the pretty moon goes.

And there we would stay
In the beautiful skies,
And through the bright clouds we would roam ;
We would see the sun set,
And see the sun rise,
And on the next rainbow come home.

LULLABY.

Sleep, my baby, sleep, my boy;
  Rest your little weary head;
'Tis your mother rocks her baby
  In his little cradle bed.

Lullaby, sweet lullaby!

(14)

LULLABY. (Page 14.)

All the little birds are sleeping,
  Every one has gone to rest,
And my precious one is resting
  In his pretty cradle nest.

Lullaby, sweet lullaby!

Sleep, O, sleep, my darling boy;
  Wake to-morrow fresh and strong;
'Tis your mother sits beside you,
  Singing you a cradle song.

Lullaby, sweet lullaby!

STOP! STOP! PRETTY WATER.

I.

" Stop ! stop! pretty water,"
  Said Mary one day,
To a frolicsome brook
  That was running away.

II.

"You run on so fast !
  I wish you would stay;
My boat and my flowers
  You will carry away.

III.

" But I will run after;
  Mother says that I may;
For I would know where
  You are running away."

IV.

So Mary ran on;
  But I have heard say
That she never could find
  Where the brook ran away.

2

MY LITTLE DOLL ROSE.

I HAVE a little doll ;
   I take care of her clothes ;
She has soft flaxen hair ;
   And her name it is Rose.

(18)

She has pretty blue eyes,
   And a very small nose,
And a cunning little mouth ;
   My dear little Rose.

I have a little sofa
   Where my doll may repose,
Or sit up like a lady ;
   My knowing little Rose.

My doll can move her arms,
   And stand upon her toes ;
Or make a pretty curtesy,
   My funny little Rose.

" How old is your dolly ? "
   Very young I suppose,
For she cannot go alone,
   My precious little Rose.

Indeed I cannot tell,
In poetry or prose,
How beautiful she is,
My darling little Rose.

"Butterflies are Pretty Things." (Page 21.)

BUTTERFLIES ARE PRETTY THINGS.

" Butterflies are pretty things,
  Prettier than you or I;
See the colors on his wings;
  Who would hurt a butterfly?

(21)

" Softly, softly, girls and boys;
   He'll come near us by and by;
Here he is, don't make a noise;—
   We'll not hurt you, butterfly."

Not to hurt a living thing,
   Let all little children try;
See, again he's on the wing;
   Good by! pretty butterfly!

OLD NURSEY.

O, HERE is papa,
　　With Edward and Jane,
Come to see good old Nursey,
　　Who lives in the lane.

(23)

She's the best of all Nurseys,
  And Edward and Jane
Love dearly good Nursey,
  Who lives in the lane.

" Here's the hen and her chickens,"
  Says Edward to Jane,
" And here's Nursey's pussy,
  That lives in the lane."

Nurse gave a good hug
  To Edward and Jane,
And told them a story
  As long as the lane.

They said, " Good by Nursey."
  She said " Come again
To see poor old Nursey,
  Who lives in the lane "

THE SUN IS UP.

THE sun is up, the sun is up,
Sing merrily we, the sun is up.
 The birds they sing,
 Upon the wing,
Hey nony nony no.

The pigeons coo,
The moolies moo,
Hey troli-loli lo.
The sun is up, the sun is up,
Sing merrily we, the sun is up.

The horses neigh,
The young lambs play,
Hey nony nony no.
The bees they hum,
O, quickly come !
Hey troli-loli lo.
The sun is up, the sun is up,
Sing merrily we, the sun is up.

The morning hours,
The dewy flowers,
Hey nony nony no,
And all we meet
Are fresh and sweet,
Hey troli-loli lo.

The sun is up, the sun is up,
Sing merrily we, the sun is up.

Then, sleepy heads,
All leave your beds!
Hey nony nony no.
For every thing
Doth sweetly sing
Hey troli-loli lo.
The sun is up, the sun is up,
Sing merrily we, the sun is up.

WALTER AND HIS DOG.

THERE was a little boy,
    And he had a piece of bread,
And he put his little cap
    On his head, head, head.

(28)

Upon his hobby horse
  Then he went to take a ride,
With his pretty Spaniel Flash
  By his side, side, side.

Little Walter was his name,
  And he said to little Flash,
" Let us gallop round the **house,**
  With a **dash, dash, dash.**"

So he laid down his bread
  In a snug little place,
And away Walter went
  For a race, race, race.

But Flash had a plan,
  In his little roguish head,
Of taking to himself
  Walter's bread, bread, bread.

So he watched for a moment
    When Walter did not look,
And the nice piece of bread
    Slyly took, took, took.

When Walter saw the rogue,
    He cried, " O, naughty Flash ; "
And he showed his little whip
    With a lash, lash, lash.

But Flash looked so good-natured,
    With his tail curled up behind,
That his aunty said to Walter,
    " Never mind, mind, mind.

" Flash is nothing but a puppy ;
    So, Walter, do not worry ;
If he knew that he'd done wrong,
    He'd be sorry, sorry, sorry ;

And don't be angry, Walter,
  That Flash has had a treat;
Here's another piece of bread
  You may eat, eat, eat."

So Walter ate his bread,
  And then to Flash he cried,
" Come, you saucy little dog,
  Let us ride, ride, ride."

IT IS A PLEASANT DAY.

Come, my children, come away,
For the sun shines bright to-day;
Little children, come with me,
Birds and brooks and posies see;
Get your hats and come away,
For it is a pleasant day.

(32)

Every thing is laughing, singing.
All the pretty flowers are springing.
See the kitten, full of fun,
Sporting in the pleasant sun.
Children too may sport and play,
For it is a pleasant day.

Bring the hoop, and bring the ball;
Come with happy faces all ;
Let us make a merry ring,
Talk, and laugh, and dance, and sing ;
Quickly, quickly, come away,
For it is a pleasant day.

3

THE GOOD MOOLLY COW.

Come! supper is ready;
   Come! boys and girls, now,
For here is fresh milk
   From the good moolly cow.

(34)

Have done with your fife,
  And your row de dow dow,
And taste this sweet milk
  From the good moolly cow.

Whoever is fretting
  Must clear up his brow,
Or he'll have no milk
  From the good moolly cow.

And here is Miss Pussy;
  She means by *mee-ow*,
Give me too some milk
  From the good moolly cow.

When children are hungry,
  O, who can tell how
They love the fresh milk
  From the good moolly cow!

So, when you meet moolly,
Just say, with a bow,
" Thank you for your milk,
Mrs. Good Moolly Cow."

NOTHING BUT BA-A. (Page 37.)

NOTHING BUT BA-A.

LITTLE Fanny and Lucy,
  One sunshiny day,
Went to walk in the meadow
  And have some play.

They said to a sheep,
  " Pray how's your mamma ? "
But the lazy sheep answered
  Them nothing but " ba-a ! "

JAMES AND HIS MOTHER.

JAMES and his mother
They loved one another,
And they went to walk one day;
And as they were walking,
And laughing and talking,
They saw some boys at play.

(38)

" Let me go ; let me run ;
Let me see all the fun ! "
Said little James then to his mother;
  " Hear them laugh, hear them shout,
  See them tumbling about,
And jumping one over the other.

  " Pray let me go too,
  O dear mother, do ! "
And Jemmie ran off to the boys ;
  He kicked, and he thumped,
  He laughed and he jumped,
He shouted and made a great noise.

  But James was so small
  That he soon got a fall,
And tumbled down into a hole ;
  He was not much hurt,
  But covered with dirt —
There Jemmie lay rubbing his poll.

His mother soon ran
To her dear little man,
Holding out to him both of her hands;
And now on the ground,
All safe and all sound,
By the side of his mother he stands.

" Never mind," said his mother ;
And they kissed one another ;
" Never mind, though you cut such a figure;
For Jemmie shall play
With the boys some day,
When he has grown older and bigger."

MASTER JOHNNY GOING TO RIDE.

Why, here's Master Johnny;
    He's taking a ride
On good Mrs. Donkey,
    With her colt by her side.

Go softly, Ma'am Donkey,
    And be sure not to trip;
And Johnny, you monkey,
    Take care of your whip.

(41)

O, LOOK AT THE MOON.

O, LOOK at the moon !
　She is shining up there;
O mother, she looks
　Like a lamp in the air.

(42)

"Oh, Look at the Moon." (Page 42.)

Last week she was smaller,
  And shaped like a bow ;
But now she's grown bigger,
  And round as an O.

Pretty moon, pretty moon,
  How you shine on the door,
And make it all bright
  On my nursery floor!

You shine on my playthings,
  And show me their place,
And I love to look up
  At your pretty bright face.

And there is a star
  Close by you, and may be
That small twinkling star
  Is your little baby.

SONG FOR A COMPANY OF CHILDREN.

CHILDREN go
To and fro,
In a merry, pretty row,
Footsteps light,
Faces bright ;
'Tis a happy sight.

(44)

Swiftly turning round and round,
Never look upon the ground,
    Follow me,
    Full of glee,
Singing merrily.

    Birds are free ;
    So are we ;
And we live as happily.
    Work we do,
    Study too,
For we learn " twice two ; "
Then we laugh, and dance, and sing,
Gay as larks upon the wing ;
    Follow me,
    Full of glee,
Singing merrily.

Work is done,
Play's begun;
Now we have our laugh and fun;
Happy days,
Pretty plays,
And no naughty ways.
Holding fast each other's **hand,**
We're a little happy band;
Follow me,
Full of glee,
Singing merrily.

THE DOG AND THE CAT,
THE DUCK AND THE RAT.

ONCE on a time in rainy weather,
  A dog and a cat,
  A duck and a rat,
All met in a barn together.

The dog he barked,
The duck she quarked,
The cat she humped up her back;
The rat he squeaked,
And off he sneaked
Straight into a nice large crack.

The little dog said, (and he looked very wise,)
"I think, Mrs. Puss,
You make a great fuss,
With your back and your great green eyes.
And you, Madam Duck,
You waddle and cluck,
Till it gives one the fidgets to hear you.
You had better run off
To the old pig's trough,
Where none but the pigs, ma'am, are near
    you."

The duck was good-natured, and she ran
    away;
  But old pussy cat
  With her back up sat,
And said she intended to stay;
  And she showed him her **paws**,
  With her long, sharp claws.
So the dog was afraid to come **near;**
  For puss, if she pleases,
  When a little dog teases,
Can give him a box on the ear.

4

TRUSTY LEARNING A B C.

" Be quiet, good Trusty ;
   See how still you can be,
For I've come to teach you
   Your A B C.

TRUSTY LEARNING A B C. (Page 50.)

" I will show you the way
    Mother reads it to me ;
She looks very sober,
    And says, A B C.

" Tom says you can't learn ;
    But father says, he
Saw a little dog once
    That knew A B C.

" So, good Trusty, attend ;
    Let us show them that we
Can learn, if we please,
    Our A B C."

To what little Frank said
    Trusty seemed to agree.
Do you think he learned much
    Of his A B C ?

DO YOU GUESS IT IS I?

I.

I AM a little thing ;
  I am not very high ;
I laugh, dance and sing,
  And sometimes I cry.

(52)

II.

I have a little head
　　All covered o'er with hair,
And I hear what is said
　　With my two ears there.

III.

On my two feet I walk;
　　I run too with ease ;
With my little tongue I talk
　　Just as much as I please.

IV.

I have ten fingers too,
　　And just so many toes;
Two eyes to see through,
　　And but one little nose.

V.

I've a mouth full of teeth,
   Where my bread and milk go in ;
And close by, underneath,
   Is my little round chin.

VI.

What is this little thing,
   Not very, very high,
That can laugh, dance, and sing ?
   Do you guess it is I ?

FIDDLEDEDEE.

Fiddledee diddledee dido,
A poor little boy he cried, O;
   He cried, for what?
   O, I've forgot;
Perhaps you had better ask Fido.

Fiddledee diddledee dido,
The dog ran off to hide, O;
   He'll bark and squeak,
   But never speak —
There's no use in asking Fido.

THE STARS AND THE BABIES.

When the stars go to sleep,
The babies awake,
And they prattle and sparkle all day;
Then the stars light their lamps,
And their playtime they take,
While the babies are sleeping away.

So good night, little baby,
  And shut up your eyes ;
Let the stars now have their turn at play ;
  They soon will begin
  To shoot through the skies,
And dance in the bright milky way.

No, no, my dear nurse,
  I cannot go to sleep ;
Since you've put the thought into my head,
  Let us have with the stars
  One game at bo-peep ;
Then good night, and a kiss, and to bed.

KITTY IN THE BASKET.

" Where is my little basket gone ? "
 Said Charlie boy one day ;
" I guess some little boy or girl
 Has taken it away.

(58)

" And Kitty too, I can't find her ;
  O, dear! what shall I do?
I wish I could my basket find,
  And little Kitty too.

" I'll go to mother's room and look;
  Perhaps she may be there,
For Kitty loves to take a nap
  In mother's easy chair.

" O mother! mother! come and look !
  See what a little heap !
My Kitty's in the basket here,
  All cuddled down to sleep."

He took the basket carefully,
  And brought it in a minute,
And showed it to his mother dear,
  With little Kitty in it.

THE FARM YARD.

THE cock is crowing,
The cows are lowing,
The ducks are quarking,
The dogs are barking,
The ass is braying,
The horse is neighing ;
Was there ever such a noise !

(60)

The birds are singing,
The bell is ringing,
The pigs are squeaking,
The barn door creaking,
The brook is babbling,
The geese are gabbling
Mercy on us, what a noise!

The sheep are ba-a-ing,
The boys ha-ha-ing,
The swallows twittering,
The girls are tittering,
Father is calling,
The cook is bawling ;
I'm nigh crazy with the noise.

Nabby is churning,
The grindstone's turning,
John is sawing,
Charles hurrahing,
Old Dobson's preaching,
The peacock's screeching ;
Who can live in such a noise !

FROLIC IN THE SNOW.

" SEE the snow ! see the snow !
  Hear the winter wind blow ;
  Make the fire burn bright ;
  Shut the doors up tight ;
  Let it storm, let it storm ;
  My Willy shall be warm."

" Dear mother, let me go
And frolic in the snow ;
'Tis so soft and so light,
So beautiful and white,
'Twill not hurt me I know ;
Let me go, let me go.

" I don't mind the cold ;
I am three years old :
Look at little Rover ;
He is powdered all over :
Let me go, let me go,
And frolic in the snow.

" I can do what Rover can ;
I am your little man ;
Let it storm, let it storm ;
I don't want to be warm ;
Dear mother, let me go,
And frolic in the snow."

SWING SWONG.

SWING swong,
Here we go ;
Sing a song,
Hurrah ho !

Swing swong,
Here we go ;
Hold in strong,
Hurrah ho !

Swing swong,
Here we go ;
Fly along,
Hurrah ho !

5 (65)

WORK AND PLAY.

COME let us take a walk, —
   The rain has gone away,—
And have some pleasant talk,
   And laugh, and sing, and play.

(66)

The old hen dries her wings,
　The young lambs frisk away
The merry sparrow sings ;
　Come let us go and play.

The brook runs gayly on
　As though it were in play,
And says to every one,
　" Let's have some fun to-day."

The little busy bee
　Doth sing and work all day,
And teaches you and me
　To work as well as play.

The world is full of flowers;
　Put up your work, I say ;
Let's use these limbs of ours
　And have some real play.

LITTLE MARY.

LITTLE Mary was good;
   The weather was fair;
She went with her mother
   To taste the fresh air.

The birds they were singing;
   Mary chatted away;
And she was as happy
   And merry as they.

LITTLE MARY. (Page 68.)

IT CAN'T BE SO.

A BOY once went the world around,
Till he a golden castle found;
    Then laughed the boy,
    Then thought the boy,
" O, were that golden castle mine,
How brightly then my house would shine!"
    O, no! O, no! O, no!
My little boy, it can't be so.

Again he went the world around,
Till he a flying pony found;
   Then laughed the boy,
   Then thought the boy,
" O, were that flying pony mine,
Then I should be a horseman fine."
   O, no! O, no! O, no!
My little boy, it can't be so.

WHEN EVENING IS COME.

WHEN evening is come,
And father's at home,
Mother says that we may
Have a go-to-bed play.
A book he will bring us,
A song he will sing us,

(71)

A story he'll tell us,
He'll make believe sell us.
And we will cut papers,
And all sorts of capers,
And laugh, dance, and play,
And frolic away,
When evening is come,
And father's at home.

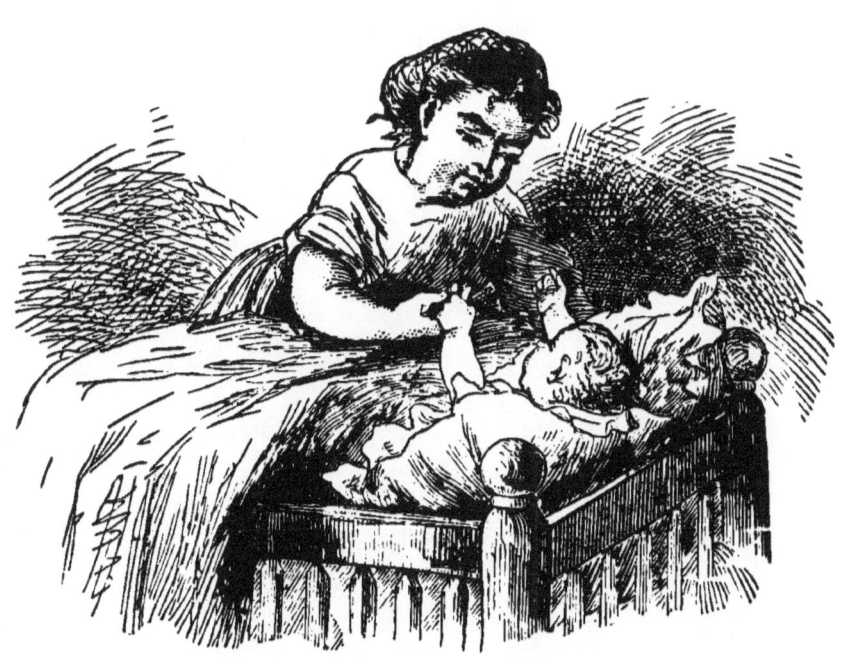

RINGELY RINGELY. (Page 73.)

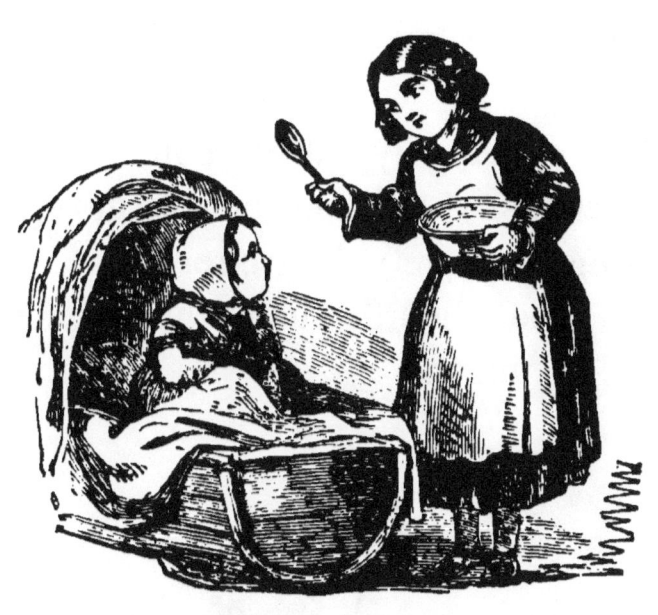

RINGELY RINGELY.

Ringely ringely dah-re-roon,
My baby has slept till almost noon,
Ringely ringely dah-re-roon,
My baby shall have his breakfast soon.

Ringely ringely dah-re-roon,
Here is his milk and here is his spoon,
Ringely ringely dah-re-roon,
He'll be a month older when comes next
    moon.

CHARLIE BOY.

O, LOOK at my hat;
   How nicely it suits!
O, look at my feet;
   I've got on new boots!

    Hurrah! for Charlie boy.

My boots they are stiff,
　My boots they are tall,
And they hold me up straight,
　So I cannot fall.

　　Hurrah ! for Charlie boy.

I'll do mother's errands
　As well as I can ;
I've got on new boots,
　And so I'm a man.

　　Hurrah ! for Charlie boy.

THE BABY'S BIRTHDAY.

Come, Charles, blow the trumpet,
And George, beat the drum,
For this is the baby's birthday!
Little Annie shall sing,
And Jemmy shall dance,
And father the jews-harp will play.
Rad-er-er too tan-da-ro te
Rad-er-er tad-or-er tan do re.

Come toss up the ball,
And spin the hum top;
We'll have a grand frolic to-day;
Let's make some soap bubbles,
And blow them up high,
And see what the baby will say.
Rad-er-er too tan-da-ro te
Rad-er-er tad-or-er tan do re.

We'll play the grand Mufti;
Let's all make a ring;
The tallest the Mufti shall play;
You must look in his face,
And see what he does,
And mind what the Mufti shall say.
Rad-er-er too tan-da-ro te
Rad-er-er tad-or-er tan do re.

And now we'll play soldiers;
All hold up your heads!
Don't you know 'tis the baby's birthday?
You must turn out your toes,
And toss your feet high;
There! this, boys and girls, is the way.
Rad-er-er too tan-da-ro te
Rad-er-er tad-or-er tan do re.

THE POOR MAN.

THE poor man is old,
   He is hungry and cold,
Let us give him some bread to eat;
   Let him come to the fire,
   Let us build it up higher,
Let us give the poor man a warm seat.

The poor man is weak ;
How pale is his cheek !
Perhaps he has met with some sorrow ;
Let us give him a bed,
Where his poor weary head
May rest, and feel better to-morrow.

DING DONG! DING DONG!

Ding dong! ding dong!
I'll sing you a song;
'Tis about a little bird;

(82)

He sat upon a tree,
And he sang to me,
And I never spoke a word.

Ding dong! ding dong!
I'll sing you a song;
'Tis about a little mouse;
He looked very cunning,
As I saw him running
About my father's house.

Ding dong! ding dong!
I'll sing you a song
About my little Kitty;
She's speckled all over,
And I know you'll love her,
For she is very pretty.

Ding dong! ding dong!
I have sung my song;
Now give me a little kiss;
I'll sing you another,
Some time or other,
That is prettier than this.

THE LITTLE BOY'S MAY DAY SONG.

" The flowers are blooming every where,
    On every hill and dell ;
And O, how beautiful they are !
    How fresh and sweet they smell !

(85)

" The little brooks, they dance along,
  And look so free and gay,
I love to hear their pleasant song ;
  I feel as glad as they.

" The young lambs bleat and frisk about,
  The bees hum round their hive,
The butterflies are coming out ;
  'Tis good to be alive.

" The trees, that looked so stiff and gray,
  With green wreaths now are hung :
O mother, let me laugh and play;
  I cannot hold my tongue.

" See yonder bird' spread out his wings,
  And mount the clear blue skies,
And mark how merrily he sings,
  As far away he flies."

" Go forth, my child, and laugh and play,
　　And let your cheerful voice
With birds, and brooks, and merry May,
　　Cry loud, Rejoice! rejoice!

" I would not check your bounding mirth,
　　My little, happy boy;
For He who made this blooming earth
　　Smiles on an infant's joy."

I.

THE sun is hidden from our sight,
  The birds are sleeping sound ;
'Tis time to say to all " Good night,"
  And give a kiss all round.

II.

Good night, my father, mother dear ;
  Now kiss your little son ;
Good night, my friends both far and near,
  Good night to every one.

III.

Good night, ye merry, merry birds;
  Sleep well till morning light;
I wish I understood your words;
  Perhaps you sing, Good night.

IV.

To all my pretty flowers, good night;
  You blossom while I sleep,
And all the stars that shine so bright
  With you their watches keep.

V.

Good night, Miss Puss; mind what I say,
  And tell it to your kittens:
When you with little children play,
  Put on your softest mittens.

VI.

Come here, my little Fido, too ;
  You always do what's right ;
I wish I was as good as you ;
  My doggie dear, good night.

VII.

The moon is lighting up the skies·
  The stars are sparkling there ;
'Tis time to shut our weary eyes,
  And say an evening prayer.

THE THREE LITTLE KITTENS.

(A Cat's Tale, with Additions.)

THREE little kittens lost their mittens;
And they began to cry,
O mother dear,
We very much fear
That we have lost our mittens.

Lost your mittens!
You naughty kittens!
Then you shall have no pie.
     Mee-ow, mee-ow, mee-ow.
No, you shall have no pie.
     Mee-ow, mee-ow, mee-ow.

The three little kittens found their mittens,
   And they began to cry,
     O mother dear,
     See here, see here;
See, we have found our mittens.
   Put on your mittens,
   You silly kittens,
And you may have some pie.
     Purr-r, purr-r, purr-r,
O, let us have the pie,
     Purr-r, purr-r, purr-r.

The three little kittens put on their mittens,
  And soon ate up the pie ;
    O mother dear,
    We greatly fear
  That we have soil'd our mittens.
    𝔖𝔬𝔦𝔩𝔢𝔡 𝔶𝔬𝔲𝔯 𝔪𝔦𝔱𝔱𝔢𝔫𝔰 !
    𝔜𝔬𝔲 𝔫𝔞𝔲𝔤𝔥𝔱𝔶 𝔨𝔦𝔱𝔱𝔢𝔫𝔰 !
  Then they began to sigh,
        Mee-ow, mee-ow, mee-ow.
  Then they began to sigh,
        Mee-ow, mee-ow, mee-ow.

The three little kittens washed their mittens,
  And hung them out to dry ;
    O mother dear,
    Do not you hear,
  That we have washed our mittens ?

Washed your mittens !
O, you're good kittens.
But I smell a rat close by :
          Hush ! hush ! mee-ow, mee-ow.
We smell a rat close by,
          Mee-ow, mee-ow, mee-ow.

(58)

COCKS AND HENS.

(To imitate the call of the fowls.)

Hen. Cock, cock, cock, cock,
I've laid an egg ;
Am I to gang bā-āre-foot ?

Cock. Hen, hen, hen, hen,
I've been up and down,

To every shop in town,
And cannot find a shoe
To fit your foot,
If I'd crow my heā-ārt out.

[To be said very quickly, except the last two words in
each verse, which are to be " screamed " out.]

www.ingramcontent.com/pod-product-compliance
Lightning Source LLC
Chambersburg PA
CBHW020803020726
47495CB00008B/2565